GUS WAS A CHRISTMAS GHOST

By JANE THAYER
PICTURES BY SEYMOUR FLEISHMAN

William Morrow and Company
New York

6 7 8 9 10
 Inquiries should be addressed to
William Morrow and Company, Inc.,
105 Madison Ave., New York, N.Y. 10016
Printed in the United States of America.
Library of Congress Catalog Card Number 77-101707

Gus was a ghost, a friendly ghost,
who lived in an attic
over the Historical Museum.
The museum was filled with ancient things
that ghosts are fond of.
There were Boston rockers,
a grandfather clock, candlestands,
oil lamps and brass candlesticks,
a spinning wheel, a music box, a harp.

Gus would have felt
right at home
except for Mr. Frizzle,
who managed the museum
with the help of the black cat Cora.
Mr. Frizzle was a splendid caretaker.
He locked the doors and windows
so burglars couldn't get in.
He put up signs saying:

NO DOGS ALLOWED

and so forth.

But Mr. Frizzle did not feel friendly
toward ghosts.
They might do some damage.
So Gus kept out of his way.
He stayed in his attic apartment all day.
He caught up on his sleep.
He sat at the window
and watched the visitors come.

Only at night,
when Mr. Frizzle closed the museum
and retired to his own apartment,
did Gus go softly downstairs.
He was joined by Cora,
who had handsome black whiskers,
white tie and boots, and topaz yellow eyes.
With Cora by his side,
Gus inspected the grandfather clock
to see if Mr. Frizzle had wound it.
He looked at the oil lamps
to see if Mr. Frizzle
was keeping the chimneys clean.

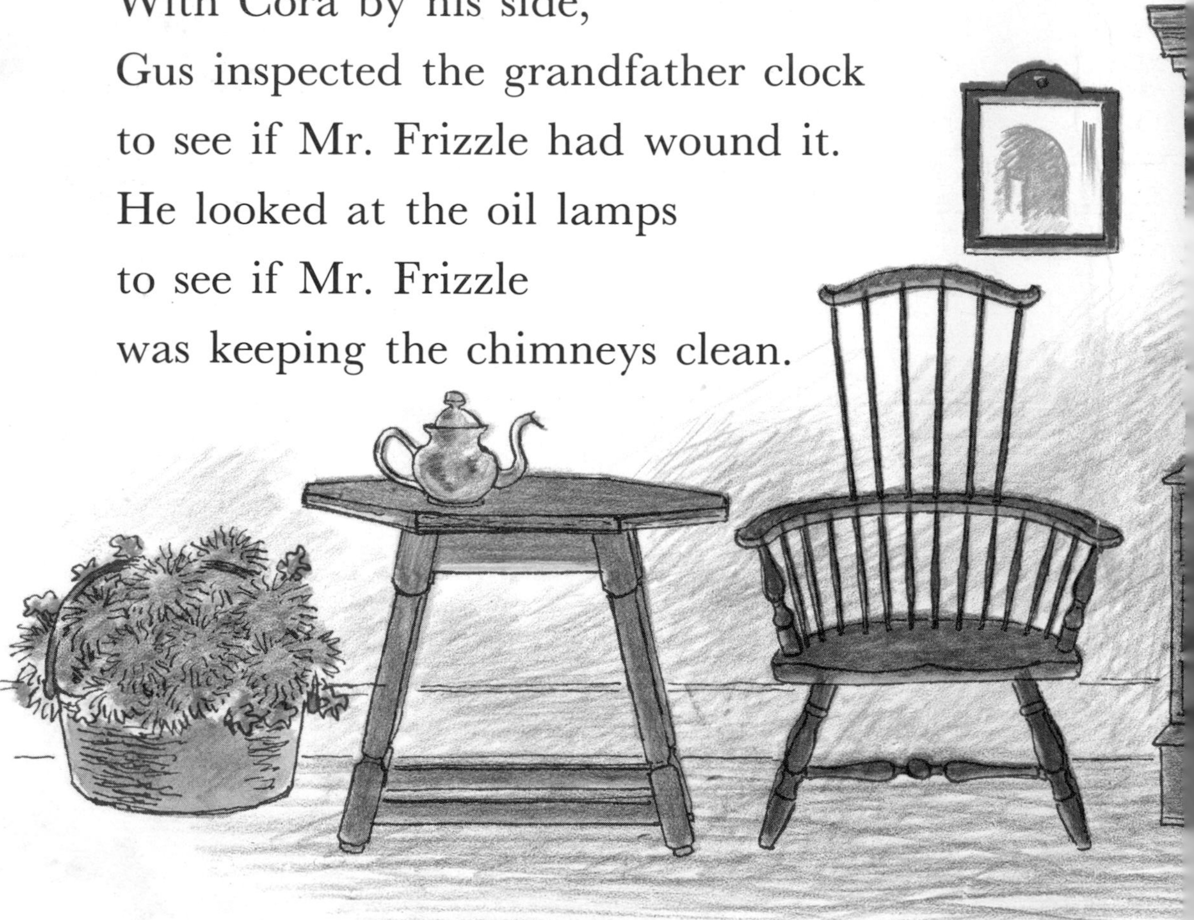

He inspected the tables for dust
and moved a washbowl and pitcher
to a better place.
“That ghost!”
complained Mr. Frizzle next morning,
moving the washbowl and pitcher back.
“He’ll break something!”

Sometimes in the night
Gus lighted the candles
in their brass candlesticks.
He built a fire in the fireplace.
He rocked in the Boston rocker
with Cora in his lap.
Mouse came out to make faces at Cora.
"He's a friend," explained Gus.

More than once Mr. Frizzle
smelled smoke and rushed down.
All he found was a Boston rocker,
gently rocking by the glowing coals,
Cora sleepily stretching,
and the candles burned down
in their candlesticks.
"That ghost!
He'll set the house on fire!"
cried Mr. Frizzle.

There were nights when Gus and Cora
went for a moonlight walk.
The door was locked,
yet Mr. Frizzle found large wet footprints
and small wet paw prints
marching across the floor.
"That ghost! Tracking up the place.
Probably left the door wide open
while he was out!"
Mr. Frizzle exclaimed.
"Mr. Frizzle is not
a friendly man,
is he, Cora?" said Gus.

When cold weather came,
Mr. Frizzle put up a sign, *Closed.*
"Now I'll get rid of that ghost, Cora!"
he said.
He put up signs saying:

That night
Mr. Frizzle heard Gus
moving the furniture around.
The next day Mr. Frizzle
put enormous padlocks on all the doors.
Gus walked in and played the harp.

Mr. Frizzle put a large trap
inside the museum door.
All he caught was Cora, livid with rage.
He built a new door marked *Ghosts Go Here.*
When Gus went through the door,
he would walk straight into a closet
where he could never get out.
Gus walked through
the closet wall.

When Mr. Frizzle peeked in,
only Mouse was there,
so mad at Mr. Frizzle
that his mustache quivered.

Mr. Frizzle furiously built a trapdoor
that would dump Gus down cellar.
Gus came right back up
and told Cora to be careful.

So busy was Mr. Frizzle trapping Gus,
that he hardly knew Christmas was coming.
Then he was invited
to spend Christmas in Florida.
"No doubt that ghost
will burn down the house
or let burglars in," he said.
"But I need a rest, and I'm going."
So Mr. Frizzle made new signs saying:

He went off the day before Christmas,
carrying his suitcase.
When Gus looked out the window
and saw Mr. Frizzle trudging away,
he hurried downstairs.
"Cora," he said, "this is Christmas Eve.
Now that Mr. Frizzle is gone,
we'll have an old-fashioned Christmas!"

"Meow?" inquired Cora with interest.
"Well, first we must hang
holly wreaths in the windows
and a large wreath trimmed with pinecones
on the door," explained Gus.
He said some ghostly words,
and the wreaths appeared.
"Doesn't that look like
an old-fashioned Christmas?" cried Gus.
"It's snowing, too."
"Meow!" said Cora.

"Now we must have a Christmas tree,"
said Gus.
He said some more ghostly words,
and in the corner
stood a beautiful tree,
its tip touching
the ceiling.
Gus went up
to the attic
and came back
draped with cobwebs,
carrying a dusty box.
They trimmed
the tree
with silver tinsel,
golden balls,
stars, angels,
and tiny candles
in holders.

"I must stuff the turkey,"
said Gus, bustling into the kitchen.
In the old kitchen,
which hadn't been used for years,
they found a twenty-pound turkey.
Gus mixed breadcrumbs
with herbs and melted butter.
He stuffed the turkey
and stored it in the old icebox
that held real ice.
"Meow?" asked Cora eagerly.
"Certainly we'll have mince pie," said Gus.
"I'll make the mincemeat."

He cooked some beef
and ground it in a meat grinder.
He put the meat in an iron kettle
with raisins, currants, citron,
chopped apples, suet, cider,
and sugar.
He set it on the wood stove,
added cinnamon
and cloves.
Gus rolled out
a piecrust.
When the mincemeat
was spicy and thick and hot,
he ladled some into the pie.
He laid on the top crust.
He cut three gashes to let out steam,
inserted a piece of macaroni
to keep the juice in,
and put the pie in the oven.

Then Gus lighted
the Christmas-tree candles.
He set a candle in every window
as a Christmas greeting to all.
"It's still snowing," said Gus.

They sat by the fire
in the light of Christmas candles,
while the music box
tinkled out *Silent Night.*

Mouse popped by,
to say hurry up with the pie.
"Meow," remarked Cora wistfully.
"Yes, it's nice and peaceful," Gus agreed.
"I almost wish Frizzle
would stay in Florida."
Suddenly Mouse muttered.
Cora narrowed
her topaz eyes.
Gus listened.
Someone was rattling the door.
"Burglars!" Gus whispered.
He braced himself against the door.
Then the burglar tried a window.
Gus rushed for a frying pan,
ready to hit him on the head.
Smash, the burglar broke the window.
Gus raised the frying pan.
The burglar began to climb in.

Suddenly Mouse snarled.
Cora cried, "Meow!"
"My goodness!" gasped Gus.
The burglar was Mr. Frizzle.
"Merry Christmas!" said Gus,
and lowered his frying pan.
Mr. Frizzle was white with snow
and his teeth chattered.
He saw Cora, her eyes wide with wonder.
"No buses running
or planes flying," he said.
"I waited hours.
I walked miles to get home.
I dropped my key in a snowdrift.
And that ghost tried to keep me out!"
"Can't he read signs?" said Gus to Cora.
Cora showed Mr. Frizzle
the sign *Beware of Burglars.*
"Har. Humpf!" said Mr. Frizzle.

"Look out!" yelled Gus,
and saved him
from going through the trapdoor.
Mr. Frizzle collapsed
in the Boston rocker beside the fire.
"Poor Frizzle," said Gus.
"He must soak his feet in mustard water,
or he'll catch pneumonia!"
He draped a cashmere shawl,
smelling of mothballs,
around Mr. Frizzle's shivering shoulders.
He brought a tub of hot water.
Mr. Frizzle put his feet in the hot water
and finally began to thaw out.
Then he noticed the Christmas tree
with all the lighted candles.
"Those candles are a fire hazard,"
said Mr. Frizzle crossly.

"Can't he see
I've got a pail of water handy?" said Gus.
"Meow," explained Cora.
"Har. Humpf!" said Mr. Frizzle.
A marvelous smell
began to drift through the room.
"Meow!" said Cora,
and Gus leaped up.
"My pie! Let's have
a piece now."

He hurried into the kitchen
and took the pie, hot, rich, meaty, spicy,
from the oven.
He cut a quarter for Mr. Frizzle,
a quarter for himself,
a piece of suitable size for Cora.
He added Vermont cheese.

He carried the plates to the fire
and dropped some crumbs for Mouse.
Mr. Frizzle, who hadn't eaten for hours,
hungrily ate his pie
and held out his plate for more.
He cleaned up every crumb.
Mouse said some people were pigs.

Finally Mr. Frizzle leaned back,
warm and full of food.
"Meow?" Cora was asking Gus.
"Yes, we'll hang up your stocking,"
said Gus.
He hung up a small sock.
"Meow!" complained Cora,
so Gus hung up a bigger sock
and left the small one for Mouse,
who muttered mousily.
Then Gus hung up Mr. Frizzle's sock.
"Meow," urged Cora.
"Oh, no," said Gus modestly,
"Santa Claus would never notice
a ghostly stocking."
"Don't you believe it," said Mr. Frizzle,
who suddenly understood
a few ghostly words.

So Gus hung up
his own ghostly sock by the fire.

"Bedtime, Cora,"
said Mr. Frizzle.
"We must come down early
and look in our stockings."
"Would it be all right
if I came too?"
Gus asked anxiously.
"Sure," said Mr. Frizzle.
Then everyone went to bed.
Gus climbed the stairs
to his attic apartment,
and as he went
he heard Mr. Frizzle say,
"Cora, I guess a ghost's
a good thing to have around."
And Cora distinctly replied,
"Merry Christmas!"

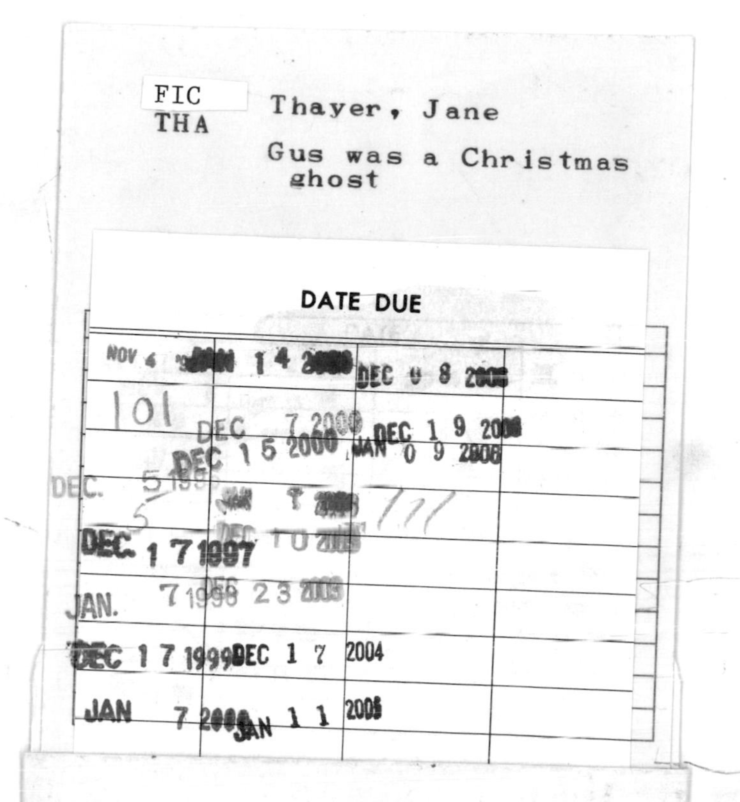
FIC
THA
Thayer, Jane
Gus was a Christmas ghost
DATE DUE
DEC 17 1999
DEC 17 2004
JAN 11 2005